Embrace

Every Facet

Embrace Every Facet

Poetry
&
Short Stories

KRISTINA MARIE DIZARD

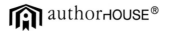

AuthorHouse™ LLC
1663 Liberty Drive
Bloomington, IN 47403
www.authorhouse.com
Phone: 1-800-839-8640

Published by AuthorHouse   02/22/2014

ISBN: 978-1-4918-6424-1 (sc)
ISBN: 978-1-4918-6425-8 (e)

Library of Congress Control Number: 2014902991

Any people depicted in stock imagery provided by Thinkstock are models, and such images are being used for illustrative purposes only. Certain stock imagery © Thinkstock.

This book is printed on acid-free paper.

Contents

Dedication

For Hannah & Mason.

You are the source of my lifelong love & inspiration.

I love you more.

Foreword

— ⁘ —

Kristina's poems and short stories vividly portray the truth of life's moments in a creatively artistic fashion. Her words display pictures that have been framed in the amazing gallery of her life.

She eloquently invites us to take our minds on a journey. Her words poetically resound like a soulful melodic tune playing a deep spiritual chorus in time. Each page flows from her heart and radiates light in darkness, peace in the midst of a storm, joy in sorrow and a faith that remains steadfast no matter what life may bring.

The virtuous nature of her written expression is fueled by a belief in a gospel of unwavering surrender, undying devotion and unconditional love. Her life is a testimony that says "I know who I am and I choose to *Embrace Every Facet.*"

Christal M.N. Jenkins, Author & Speaker

Discovering the True Love Within, LIVE! and God Crazy Freedom

Introduction

Even at a young age my soul longed for the sweetness of solitude. For as long as I can remember I have craved the opportunity to be alone with my thoughts, free-flowing words and a pen. When I was eight I would climb a tree in the front yard to escape the life beneath it. I would carelessly climb to the very tip top and sit for hours. A new world emerged. It's interesting how some view solitude as a curse, yet others long in adoration for its fleeting presence.

One should never be embarrassed to be alone; you are after all, great company. If we are not secure or self aware with our own being, how can we view the world without distorted lenses? We must remember, true vision requires more than merely sight.

A mistake we often make is assuming that solitude is synonymous for quietness. For in those moments of solitude we may be externally quiet, however our internal noise and dialogue is crucial. As we spend moments alone self-awareness creeps in like the brisk cold air on a chilly day; typically un-invited.

I pray that we all embrace this beautiful, life-long journey of self-discovery, despite how many blankets are required along the way.

Part 1: Soul.

_____ ⚬⚬ _____

Hesed.

Embody.

wife-mother-lover-teacher

banker-painter-friend-preacher

must we just pick one?

surgeon-gypsy-grandma-dancer

barista-operator-aunt-romancer

to embrace every facet is much more fun

Path.

The walks of our lives all differ, even when on similar trails -
bravely following the path of our heart ensures we never fail.

Shine. (for Julie)

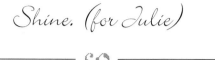

It matters not where you're from or what you have been through; if a diamond from the dirt can shine so bright, my love then so can you.

When a man walks.

———— ❦ ————

She says there's something about when a man walks

Confident air swaggers, birds halt, sounds swell

Pavement shakes, effortless rhythm, a kind smell

She says there's something about when a man walks

Train of your past.

———————— ∽ ————————

If you're on the "what if" or "if only" train
I suggest getting off at the next stop.

Dance.

Our lives are a unique & beautiful dance to which we must not step faster or slower than the music of our souls.

Act.

Compassion acts

Without judgment

Without pre-requisites

Without a second thought

Compassion acts

Love.

Love is its own art form; it cannot be defined or stifled.

Fly.

Like an eagle spreading its wings

I am ready for take off

To see clearly amidst the high clouds

Like an instrument finely tuned

Now shining and polished

My voice has become quite loud

Like a tree standing tall

Embrace the storm I will

Never shaken, stirred or blown

Like a caterpillar transformed

I fight my nerves

Boldly braving the unknown

Like a painter gone mad

I cherish every stroke of the brush

Errors add to its rare authentic beauty

Like a mysterious rainbow

Glowing bright amidst the haze

You'll never discover all of me

Kristina Marie Dizard

Empty.

Trying to love someone before you love yourself is like handing an empty glass to one who is thirsty.

The city.

Fog lays itself down, covered in mystery am I

Stars lit up shine n' sparkle just for me

Waterfall singing nearby begs me to dance

Tonight, I am romanced by the sweet city

W[hole].

Covering her skin with traces of deep love,
his touch penetrates deep into her soul.

Yet scars from her past rise up & ache.
Contradiction: She is with holes & yet whole.

Intimacy.

Sitting alone in silence with someone can reveal to you, at times, more than the lengthiest of conversations.

Light.

I choose to flutter near the light—although I may get burned

For it beats a life in darkness—this my friends I've learned

Vision.

True vision requires more than sight and blindness
is inevitable if we surrender to fright.

Every foreign land.

You

You can't define me

Go ahead keep on tryin'

Watch my every move

You

You can't define me

Go ahead keep on tryin'

What are you trying to prove?

You

You can't define me

Go ahead keep on tryin'

Don't I fit into your conforming box?

You

You can't define me

Go ahead keep on tryin'

You look pretty frail to be throwin' such big rocks

You

You can't define me

Go ahead keep on tryin'

I've more sides than a diamond so rare

Kristina Marie Dizard

You

You can't define me

Go ahead keep on tryin'

You think your lookin' right at me, am I really there?

You

You can't define me

Go ahead keep on tryin'

Hard to observe and judge something so free

You

You can't define me

Go ahead keep on tryin'

Look again and tell me, now what do you see?

You

You can't define me

Go ahead keep on tryin'

A different side, undefined now you understand

You

You can't define me

Go ahead keep on tryin'

I am the beauty in every foreign land

Kristina Marie Dizard

Cement.

———————— ⚮ ————————

The cold cement dries

without fail, splitting

cracks remain forevermore.

Stop sweeping.

Never have so much repressed emotion swept under the rug that you can't move forward without stumbling.

Fall.

I am a tree in the prime of fall.

Embracing my nakedness I stand
vulnerable for all to see.

Strong.

Rooted.

Fearless.

I am a tree in the prime of fall.

Insomnia.

--- ❦ ---

sing the sweet song

of sleep awake I lay

all night long sleepy-weeping

dreams come not

tales told 'n untold

eyes closed awake-stinging

rolled and tossing

tight silk slinkin'

comfort a key with no lock

cold and bitter

pressure n' push

away keep the tickin-tock

File cabinet.

If you continue to file away thoughts & emotions you'll find, in 20 years, a cabinet full of repressed paperwork.

Dream carnival.

— ✆ —

Little one's laughing-crafting and clapping-
cotton candy stuck-sticking goo.

Painted faces singing-chatting-remembering,
elephants ear one or two?

Twirling and leaping-heaping and dancing,
sunny day at the fair with mom blue.

Sipping and savoring-clowns layering
soaked in funny-freckled mirror glue.

Tide.

———————— ❧ ————————

Sometimes the waves in our lives carry such a persistent, natural strength that we are forced to let go & embrace the rhythm of the tide.

Simple things.

———————— ⧉ ————————

Be a lover of life and all that's in it

By day and by night it's the simple things

A smile carries on shining with the sun

Music resonates n' shakes your soul

The smell of the oceans tide runs deep

Wind breaks the earth with complete control

Leaves rise up and freely dance

Chatter in the bank carries its own rhythm

An innocent face with crayons spreads cheer

Birds flying high dare us to come with 'em

Be a lover of life and all that's in it

By day and night it's the simple things

Kristina Marie Dizard

Clarity.

It's hard on the days filled with foggy flashbacks to envision the future with clarity.

For if our minds remain blurred and reminiscent, what can we claim to see clearly?

Embrace.

Leaves dance slowly,

awaiting embrace from the crisp

vulnerable wind.

Web.

Untangling yourself from a web of manipulation is similar to that of a spider. Despite thorough efforts to brush it off, fear remains that traces of the web still linger.

Ignorance.

It is a humbling day when one realizes the devastation
of the title wave caused by their ignorance.
Sadly, the ripple effects are still yet to come.

Adventure awaits.

———————— ✑ ————————

The wind is my embrace today - while
some scurry about I choose to play

Leaves dance freely, the sun sneaks a smile - I'll
travel not by car but mind, mile after mile

A journey within, adventures calling - whispering
my name with each rain drop that's falling

Monotony and day-to-day do not stir the soul - why
waste time doing only what's expected or told?

We only have one life and I'll do as I please - dance
in the rain, twirl about and laugh with ease

Let's lighten up lovely ones, this life's awaiting
you—stop, listen, and follow your inner truth

Gold.

It may be broken into pieces but see how it still shines; that piece of gold although damaged remains a valuable find.

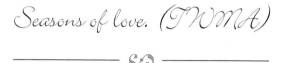

Seasons of love. (TWMA)

In the warm glow of the noon day sun,
our love will brilliantly shine.

In the rustle of the crisp autumn
leaves our love will dance.

In the passion of the roaring tides our love will sing.

In the glory of the majestic mountaintops
our love will forever triumph.

Harmony.

If we can fine tune the art of living in balance, the sweet harmony of our lives will precede us.

Floodgate.

I choose to open the floodgate of my mind
and swim with my deepest fears.

Quiet compass.

The quietness in my soul echoes throughout the
house—emptiness rings, searching its whereabouts

Silence swiftly stiffens, uneasy with peace-
barrenness flows freely from my neck to my knees

I embrace divine days where the inner compass
turns quietly - remnants of sweet silence
remain & truth is revealed mightily

Mine.

The beauty I proudly hide

    deeper than between my thighs

The mystery that clings on tight

    never found you search all night

The love that speaks from my eyes

    reaches out n' felt in the tides

The reflection of my bare soul seen

    draws you near and in-between

For Michael.

A gentle soul that flew high with laughter,
literature and love—has left this earth and
joined others in the glistening light above.

A place erupting with love.

Of course he would travel there at an age we
all despaired—for the finest kind souls leave
imprints of fondness & return into thin air.

Deep, warm chestnut eyes and a smile forever
unmatched—we adore you dear brother and will
always remember cherished games of catch.

Amongst the many things you left us, the greatest
being memories of love—we still ache for you
yet know, you're belly laughing up above.

Part 2: Sprirt.

———————— ∽ ————————

Yasha.

Grip.

He never lets go, His tight grip is fixed on His creation

With unfailing love and determination

Stronger He holds His perfectly
molded sons and daughters

Filling the open aching wounds of
absent mothers and fathers

Set the bar.

———————— ⟋⟍ ————————

Never feel guilty ladies about setting the bar
so high that no man can attain it without
endurance and help from the divine.

Stand.

———————— ✑ ————————

Stand still amidst the storm that's brewing all around

Plant your weathered, beautiful
feet firmly on solid ground

Lift up those weary, trembling hands,
surrender through it all

Combat the guilt and shame that
clings, for even the best fall

Disaster blowing, heartache
raining & indecisive winds

Shall not stop us from embracing the
disaster and continuing to praise Him

Despite the passing, deceptive havoc,
several things remain true

Of those the most important is: He
loves & has a plan for you

Kristina Marie Dizard

Redemptive love.

———————— ⚭ ————————

Wrong or right matters not

True love exemplified

In the end just one thing matters

For you both He died

In love.

I am in love, it doesn't come and go

I am in love, watch it be forever so

Not in love with fallacies, ambiguities or a need to please

But with my Maker, my Healer, the
one I come to on my knees

I am in love, it doesn't come and go

I am in love, watch it be forever so

Live.

⸺ ⸺ ❦ ⸺ ⸺

A bird chirps softly, the light glistens through

Morning has eagerly come, and we've been given a new

A new day to live, love and pray

A new day to make an impact, but also play

Life will continue, ready or not

Don't be anxious love, you're all He wants

He wants you to surrender your will to His

Trusting and enjoying, for it's your life to live

So be aware, be present and stand

No matter what, He's holding your hand

His grip is tight, if anyone to choose

You want Him by your side, He doesn't lose

His grip never weakens, waivers or slips

Whatever is burdening you, He will fix

We can live life and enjoy this journey

What's the point if you're always in a hurry?

Live every breath to the fullest,
whether you feel joy or pain

No matter what the situation, glorify His name

So let go, shake loose, you have been set free

I'm glad to tell you love; He died for you and me

Kristina Marie Dizard

Peace.

There's a peace you'll only find

When you surrender all; heart, soul & mind

His peace can saturate through

All oppressing or troubling you

Only in surrendering all to Him

Will you truly find peace within

Refuge.

God's mercy and grace wash over
us, even when we see no need

For He knows the desires of our
hearts & the sin as well He sees

Un-deserving we feel at times as His children
bow'd heads and shamed hearts

Yet He gently embraces us with the wind
and inevitably the healing starts

Receiving His love so freely is at
times not an easy task

We need not sweat and toil, for
our works He does not ask

He longs for us to be His hands and
feet, extending His love to all

It's time to forgive yourself friend,
for even the best fall

This life's a large journey of small
decisions, listening to Him each day

Simplifies the once complex and
draws near the light of day

Storm.

When hefty winds blow & waves are tossed like
the storm on the Sea of Galilee, what one must
remember is in trusting Him there is perfect peace.

Send me, Lord.

———— ⟨⟩ ————

You say come to me all who are thirsty,
yet some do not know the path

Help me lead them Lord, so their sorrows shall not last

Let me be a hand to the needy, eye to the
blind and joy to those that mourn

Use me to be Your hands and feet,
repairing that which is torn

I am willing, and see myself as no
greater than any other man

Change lives, heal the broken-hearted,
freedom for captives is the plan

The harvest is great yet the workers are
few, I am willing & ready to serve

For compassion, mercy, grace and love is only a
small portion of what Your people deserve

Red as scarlet.

Oh precious daughter, who knows not her worth

Have no doubt child, I knew you before your birth

The strands of hair on your head I
have numbered with care

My longing is for you to know Me, for I was there

There when you compromised your
body, where My spirit resides

Taken for granted by this world full of lust and pride

Nothing makes you feel better love, but I know what can

My daughter; you are hopelessly looking to man

I am your Father, Creator and the one who saves

There is no need to live any longer like a slave

To your past, your pain, your false identity

For all that you truly are, mirrors Me

Your sins red as scarlet, I have made white as snow

Open your eyes and look up, for it
is I you must get to know

Rest.

Let us learn to rest in You

Quiet the clutter of the world

To hear Your voice, discern Your sprit

To use our sword and shield

Continually walking in shoes of peace

Harnessed with the belt of truth

How important it is to learn to rest

Even in our innocent youth

The breastplate of righteousness is our friend

Reminding us who we are

If we walk, fully armed in You

We have Your peace amidst any righteous war

Quilt.

I am a quilt made with the fabric of grace, woven together with the needle of God's faithfulness.

Reigning grace.

———— ∽ ————

Waves of grace wash over us, even without our knowing.

Crashing into the banks of our past—
grace now overflowing.

Seeping and soaking into our souls,
refreshing and cleansing us through.

You need not strive to earn it; simply
let His grace rain down on you.

Every righteous war.

—————————— ☙ ——————————

Raise you head high, look down no longer child

He has made you complete in His
image that knows no shame

Wipe those tears, weep no more

He binds up the broken-hearted, just call on His name

Gird up your strength, fight for your freedoms

He is your strength and shield for every righteous war

Love yourself, draw blood no more love

He's shed enough, He doesn't need more

Put the bottle down, stop drinking in vain

He says come to me all who are thirsty, He will satisfy

Break free from those chains you know so well

He sets the captives FREE

Again I tell you my dear friend; He died for you and me

Kristina Marie Dizard

Balance.

As you walk barefoot on the logs by the shore remember the path of your life requires a similar, delicate balance.

Choosing love.

Love is always a choice, regardless of how we may feel
Following Gods command is at times a test of will

This doesn't mean blind ignorance,
or a stepping stool to be

Simply remember to act in love &
your heart shall be forever free

Grace.

Crisp wind against my face—hovering
around as does His grace.

Blowing freely for all to receive—all
that's required is repent & believe.

Faithful.

Stepping out in faith may intimidate,
yet Gods word remains true

Fret not for doubting; simply
remember all He's done for you

From simple to complex, He changes
lives, heals wounds & releases joy

Through your fears the truth remains:
He is faithful to every girl and boy

The Land of In-between.

—— ❧ ——

Where the death of old dreams meets hope unseen.

I'm stuck in the land of in-between.

Everything's muted & shades of gray,
black and white feel so far away.

I'm stuck in the land of in-between.

Only yesterday it seemed there was
no such thing, as in-between.

Now I know, inevitably the trees and flowers grow.
We have no say-so. Evolving begins; a shedding of old
skin means beauty inevitably revealed from within.

Now I stand, naked & vulnerable yet completely
able of escaping this foreign grey in-between.

One thing I demand and freely receive is that
He holds my hand as I laugh & still grieve
yes I'll escape this land of in-between.

And enter into the land of the free . . .

A bit more.

———————— ⟡ ————————

Despertar.

Lost traveler.

―――――――――― ᘒ ――――――――――

After months of planning, a curious bright-eyed traveler and her seasoned guide committed to an adventure together. A glistening mountain top awaited them as they set out for the journey of a lifetime. About halfway up the mountain the traveler had to take a break, she was getting weary from the intense climbing and thick heat. After taking a sip of water she glanced up and noticed her guide was gone. Immediate fear and panic swept over her blushed body as she pondered what to do. She stood up onto her wobbly feet and realized she didn't know where to go. She scratched her insecurities as if they were the chicken pox. Give up and go back down the mountain, or continue to climb it alone? As she took one last glimpse at the promise that awaited her she decided to keep climbing, even if it meant braving the unknown alone and creating a new path.

Perception.

———————— ∽ ————————

As young Sam approached the car each step required more effort than the last. He looked weary, as if he was breaking at the seams.

"I just don't get it!" Sam cried. Ali and Mandalita looked at each other, their dancing eyes deciding who would speak.

"What is it Sam? What happened at school that has you so upset?" Mandalita, their nanny questioned.

"At school, the teacher showed us these pictures that she called art, and to me, they were nothing. I don't see the big deal Mandalita; it's just stupid splotches of paint. They didn't even look like anything, just lines and big, messy splashes of color."

As they pulled into the driveway Ali ran up to her room to change for her driving class that began shortly. Mandalita and Sam continued their conversation. Chaos and perfection intersected as he dropped his weathered backpack on the finely polished hardwood kitchen floor.

"Did you tell your teacher that Sam?"

"Well she asked what we thought, and everyone said these

great, clever things and I was quiet when it was my turn and then they all laughed at me! She said I need to work on opening my eyes if I couldn't see it. What does that even mean?"

"When you saw what she showed you, why do you think you were not able to see the 'mess' as beautiful or some form of art?" Mandalita asked as she knelt beside him.

He lifted his bright, distressed almond eyes up toward Mandalita; she was patiently waiting for his reply.

"Once I made this super big cardboard house from scratch, measured the walls and windows, painted it and everything, Ali helped me." His words fumbled out between sobs.

"Mom made me throw it away before dad came home and got angry about the mess I had made. I don't know what made me think of that." Sam's head sunk down and the waterfall of tears had stopped.

"To me, if it was art, mom wouldn't hate it. I guess art can't really look messy."

Mandalita held a sad look in her captivating eyes. She tied up the garbage bag in the kitchen and began to walk outside to take out the trash before Kate came home. Unsure if their father would be joining them for dinner, she wanted to make sure everything was picked up. Mandalita nodded for Sam to come with her to finish their conversation. It was raining outside, naturally Sam hesitated.

"It's just rain Sam." Her smirk dared him to come along.

He smiled, accepted her dare and followed her out the stained glass door that was imported from Italy. Ali told Mandalita it had taken their mom 5 agonizing weeks (which included getting the input of all the neighbors) to decide on a design for the door.

The rain fell heavily, each drop releasing its own unique sound, determined to reach its appointed destination. Mandalita smiled, closed her eyes and surrendered, letting her head of long dark hair fall back. A large, flirtatious drop of rain kissed her full pomegranate lips and gracefully slid down her chin, neck and then disappeared into her flesh.

Getting impatient Sam grabbed the garbage bag from her hands as her eyes were still closed and took it down the street to the garbage can. He hated getting wet.

Mandalita finally opened her eyes and watched Sam hurry towards her; he made no effort to disguise his hatred for the same rain Mandalita adored.

"C'mon, I am cold and getting so wet!"

Mandalita smiled at him as rain dripped off her chin and nodded in agreement. Just as they both turned around to head into the house they heard a startling crash.

"Oh no!"

"The garbage!" Worried Sam.

It had been blown over by a rough, mischievous gust of

wind that had not quite finished playing. Such a thick breeze you could almost see it smiling and dancing about. Sam ran back over to the garbage can.

"Sam, no!"

Mandalita ran after him in her bare feet and held her petite hand out to stop him. It was the first time he had heard her raise her usually delicate voice.

"You see, your first instinct is to just stop it and clean it up right away. Just wait a minute and watch!" She demanded.

Confused, Sam looked at her, and then the trash on the ground.

The white garbage bag had ripped and flowing out of it was left over spaghetti sauce. The thick sauce slid slowly and gracefully down the glistening cement. Then a thin stream of dense white liquid, (probably the egg whites that had expired) appeared. They blended in with the sauce perfectly. Different stunning shades of reds and pinks blended together blissfully before their eyes.

"You see Sam, this right here . . . is art. Messy, yet beautiful; the cement is your canvas. Do you see it?"

The rain was still pouring, adding final impressionistic touches to its masterpiece.

She knelt down, pushed his thick, wet hair to the side and whispered into his small cold ear,

"Your teacher is wrong Sam. You have fine eyes, they are just fine."

She encouraged him as she slid her damp finger over his left eyelid.

"The problem you are having, it's in your mind."

Balance.

—————— ✑ ——————

His suit was crisp and the smell of the daily paper empowered him as he strolled into the building that housed him for at least ten hours every day. At times throughout the workday he peered at himself through the reflections of the mirrored windows and wondered about the man he saw. He wondered why he stepped onto that hamster wheel daily and was missing his sons' first words, steps and future treasured memories. Surely his family needed the income he brought in, and he worked this hard because he loved them. Those words kept running through his mind and fueling him forward for years, but not without a price.

A few years later he ran across a picture that his son had drawn that he had never seen before. It was of him, at the top of a ladder and his son and wife at the bottom. Smiles were on their faces, yet his was stern. At the top of the ladder and drawing there was nothing else, only vast emptiness. The bottom of the drawing his wife was hugging their son and it was filled with joy, pets and flowers. It was then that he had this life-changing thought: I wonder if the lonely view from the top of the esteemed corporate ladder has been worth the climb? Then he realized, most falls happen at the top, yet the center is where one achieves the greatest balance.

A time to rest.

———————— ⟋⟍ ————————

Two young hikers arrogantly passed a resting, elderly gentleman on their way up the mountain and chuckled, "Man, if I ever have to sit and rest during a hike like him, shoot me!" One condescendingly voiced to the other as they hissed by. The old man heard, but let the jagged words drip off his body instead of penetrate into his soul. He waited another few minutes and then continued up the beckoning mountain. Several minutes later the gray-haired grandfather passed the boys and they quickly swapped out their panting for humble smiles. The vocal one from prior suddenly had no words as his pride swiftly kidnapped his voice. However his friend spoke up, "Hey mister, no offense, but how can you handle this?" he pants. "My son, you have yet to discover the art of discerning the time to rest in this journey of life, versus the time to climb." With that sentence he strolled by, and continued uphill in his pursuit of natures mysteries.

Thread of humanity.

———————— ❦ ————————

"I remember the first time we met; I pray I will never forget it." The young student shares with his Professor over coffee.

"She was nervous, as was I for our first day. Our eyes met swiftly as we sat down for class. The kindness in her soul radiated through her green apple eyes. Although her lips were slow to smile, I know inside her heart was racing." Scott's eyes are filled with tears that hold memories; therefore he tries with all his might to stop them from escaping.

"How can you be sure her heart was racing?" The Professor questions out of sheer curiosity. He has removed his thick glasses as he listens to Scott, one of his brightest students who has been absent for several days.

"Oh I just know . . . " Again, the moist memories threaten to abandon their home as he tears up.

"We spent the remainder of that crisp fall season embracing one another with the same natural ease as the wind hugs the trees. I opened my heart and let her in deeper than anyone else." He looks up at his Professor and searches for a glimpse of validation or understanding.

"She understood my soul . . . never expected me to be

anything other than true to myself. It was miraculous. Now it's over. I . . . " Scott begins shaking his head as he struggles to believe that what was once his reality are now merely flashes of memories to reminisce upon.

The Professor chimes in, "All of humanity is tied together by the common thread of true love, aren't we?" He inquires. "Regardless of circumstance, we all have our stories Scott, and I am sorry to hear that your heart is having such a hard time."

"True love . . . " Scott mumbles, "If you ask me, that term seems like an oxy-moron. No such thing really exists. I thought I had it, but how can it be true if it evaporates and disappears?"

The Professor attempts to tread lightly, "Well simply because water can eventually evaporate into air does not mean it was not once water . . . right?"

"I understand what you are saying Professor, and I appreciate you listening, but I am not holding onto my thread any longer. Actually, I feel as though I am at the end of my rope and have decided to let go of love all together."

"Well, that's the beauty of it Scott, even when you feel like letting go, something much larger than either one of us is holding on to the other end of that rope." The professor looks directly into Scotts eyes as he witnesses the first victorious tear escape down his weary face. He continues, "Let go Scott, release the heaviness of your heartbreak and I promise you will be ok. We are all strung together into an intricate web of love and grace from which you cannot fall, even upon letting go."

Two paths.

———————— ✧ ————————

"I've had enough!" Andrew yelled as he threw a brittle, thin stick into the bushes. The thick wind hissed back, challenging his temper. Determined, forceful raindrops raged to the ground and dampened his clothing and backpack quicker than he could have if he'd tried.

"This storm is making it impossible for me to make any real progress." He angrily mumbled to himself.

As his eyes rose up from the glistening rocks and muddy path he was on he noticed a different trail nearby. He approached it.

"I wonder why I didn't see this before . . ." His inner dialogue quickly became shared.

"Well hello there, my name's Jack." Jacks coarse hand reached out with expectation. His old, foggy blue eyes held many secrets and his crooked smile shone amidst the dark storm clouds.

"Jack, I'm Andrew, pleasure. I'm curious where this trail goes?" His eyes sparkled with curiosity as he continued, "You know, if I am being honest, this path I have been on heads uphill and is too rigorous for me to keep traveling.

This one you're on seems to eventually take me to the same place, right?" Andrews question was filled with such hope it felt more like a statement.

"You know son, I can't say for sure. But I do know that path you're on is a toughie. Took mighty strength for me to finish out that one when I was young. But I did it." Jack glanced at the trail. "Oh I see, this storm's making it harder isn't it? Them trees and steep hills don't do so well when the weathers acting up."

"Exactly my point Jack. This path looks simpler, and hardly has any hills. The trees are pushed back farther and it's going to be much easier for me to just take this route. Do you mind if I join you Jack?" Andrew picked up his dripping backpack and threw it over his shoulder.

"Now son, wait just a minute." Jacks eyes opened up, as if they were about to reveal one of his many tucked away secrets. "This path may be simpler, but it ain't yours. Despite them harsh weather conditions and uphill climbin' that paths got something it wants to reveal to you as you fight through it and finish what you started. I know the path, just like the one of our lives, gets mighty cluttered at times. You gotta just clean it up as best you can as you go. As tempting as this simpler path seems, you have to remember that if you ain't gonna follow your path in this life son, even when it seems impossible, then who will?"

Kristina Marie Dizard

Notes